Publisher's Cataloging-In-Publication Data

McGranaghan, John.
Saturn for my birthday / by John McGranaghan ; illustrated by Wendy Edelson.
p. : col. ill. ; cm.
Summary: Jeffrey wants the planet Saturn for his birthday, along with all 47 of its moons.
He plans to share his present with friends at school and his teacher, Mrs. Cassini.
"For Creative Minds" section includes fun facts about Saturn and the Solar System.
Interest age level: 004-008.
Interest grade level: P-3.
ISBN: 978-1-934359-13-6 (hardcover)
ISBN: 978-1-934359-27-3 (pbk.)

1. Saturn (Planet)--Juvenile fiction. 2. Solar system--Juvenile fiction. 3. Birthdays--Juvenile fiction.
4. Saturn (Planet)--Fiction. 5. Solar system--Fiction. 6. Birthdays--Fiction. I. Edelson, Wendy. II. Title.

PZ7.M168 Sat 2008
[E]   2008920382

Printed in China

Sylvan Dell Publishing
976 Houston Northcutt Blvd., Suite 3
Mt. Pleasant, SC 29464

Thanks to Lawrence Dewarf, Astronomy
Professor at Villanova University for his help.
Inspired by John & Kyle, dedicated to Mom &
Dad, made possible by Dina—JM

In loving memory of my son, Gabriel Merlin
Kosdan, and to the bright and shining promise
of Aidan and Levi—WE

Thanks to educators at NASA/JPL (Jet
Propulsion Laboratory) for verifying the
accuracy of the information in this book.

"I know what I want," said Jeffrey as he marched into the kitchen. "But don't worry Dad; it's not another pet."

"Good. We have enough animals around here already. So what'll it be?"

"Saturn!"

Milk squirted out of his Dad's nose. "The planet?"

"Yeah Dad, I want Saturn, and don't forget the moons: all forty-seven of them. I want Saturn for my birthday, with the moons included."

"But Saturn is millions of miles away," said Dad.

"I know. That's why you have to order it right away. Mrs. Cassini taught us all about Saturn in school. The closest it comes to Earth is about 800 million miles, and that's still pretty far, so it might take a little while to get here."

"And Saturn is almost 900 million miles from the sun, so it's really, really cold— about 200 degrees below zero.

"But don't worry. As soon as I get Saturn home, I'll wrap a blanket around it, and we'll sit in front of the fireplace. I'll even put a towel underneath, in case it has to go . . . melt a little. We'll watch TV, maybe the science channel, until it's time for bed.

"Then we'll go upstairs and take a nice warm bath."

"You cannot put Saturn in the tub, Jeffrey."

"Yes I can, Dad. Mrs. Cassini said Saturn could float. I'll get in first, and then I'll put Saturn in. I'll clean it up and I'll wash everywhere, even between the rings, until Saturn's all shiny and yellow."

"And when it's time for bed, I won't need any more night lights. Saturn's moons will light up my room! I'll put Titan right above my bed since it's the biggest moon."

"I'll put Pandora next to my toy box, Calypso by my radio, and Janus above the doorway. Atlas will go right next to my globe, Tethys by my fish tank, and I'll put Mimas next to my rock collection.

"I'll line up all the other moons on my desk. Before going to bed, I'll say good night to each one. I'll make up names for the new moons that just have numbers—really cool names like Orbiter and Royce.

"And in the morning, when I wake up, I'll take Saturn to school. I'll even share Saturn with the other kids. I'll give everyone in my class one of Saturn's rings. That's okay because Mrs. Cassini said Saturn has lots of rings.

"I'll give one to my best friend Tommy so he can roll it around the schoolyard at recess. And I'll give one to Kara because she loves to hula hoop. I'll even give Mrs. Cassini a ring. No, I'll give her three rings! Then she'll have one for each ear and one to wear as a bracelet."

"Jeffrey, Saturn is not a toy. It's a planet."

"And it's an old planet, Dad, about four-and-a-half billion years old. So I promise to take really good care of it. I won't leave it out in the rain. When I'm done playing with it, I'll always put it away. I'll keep Saturn in my room, right next to . . ."

"Wait a minute Jeffrey, you can't have Saturn."

"Come on Dad, please."

"No,"

"But Dad, I really really want it. Why not?"

"Saturn is too big!"

"You mean it won't fit in my room?"

"Exactly. Saturn is enormous. It's the second biggest planet in the solar system."

"Oh yeah, that's right. Mrs. Cassini did say Saturn is nine times bigger than Earth. Maybe I should get something a little smaller."

"Now you're talking," said Dad.

"How about one of the moons?" asked Jeffrey. "Maybe Mimas?"

"No Jeffrey, that's still too big. No moons! No planets! No stars! Nothing from outer space. Your present must be something from planet Earth and something we can fit inside this house."

"Hmmm . . .," thought Jeffrey . . .

"I know! How about a puppy? I'll call him Saturn."

For Creative Minds

Solar System Fun Facts

Did you know that the sun is a star and that we live on a planet?

There are eight planets that orbit around the sun. Moons orbit around the planets.

We live on Earth, the third planet from the sun. Saturn is the sixth planet from the sun and is easily recognizable because of its bright, colorful rings.

The planets in order of their distance from the sun are: Mercury, Venus, Earth, Mars, Jupiter, Saturn, Uranus, and Neptune.

We used to think there was a 9th planet named Pluto, but it's actually one of more than 40 "dwarf planets" that orbit our sun.

An asteroid belt, the dwarf planets, and comets also orbit the sun.

Most meteors are "space dust" from the comet tails.

We have 24 hours in a day because it takes the Earth 24 hours to rotate on its axis.

It only takes Saturn 10 hours and 39 minutes to rotate on its axis. A "day" on Saturn would be less than 11 hours!

It takes the Earth 365 days, one year, to revolve around the sun. It takes Saturn 10,759 Earth days to revolve around the sun. If you divide 365 into 10,759, how many Earth years does it take for Saturn to revolve around the sun?

Saturn Fun Facts:

Giovanni Domenico Cassini, also known as Jean-Dominique Cassini, was a 17th century astronomer who discovered four of Saturn's moons and a space between two of Saturn's rings, which is called the Cassini Division. Although Cassini was married, there is no evidence that Mrs. Cassini was Jeffrey's teacher.

Saturn is yellow when viewed from space.

Saturn is approximately 4.5 billion years old—the same age as the sun, the Earth and the rest of the planets.

The Cassini-Huygens is a cooperative project among NASA, the European Space Agency, and the Italian Space Agency. The Cassini spacecraft was launched on October 1997. It arrived at Saturn in July 2004 to study the planet for four years.

Saturn is one of the brightest lights in the night sky and can be easily seen without a telescope. If you use a telescope though, you can see the rings.

The ancient Romans named Saturn after their god of agriculture. Saturday was named after him too.

Saturn's Size:

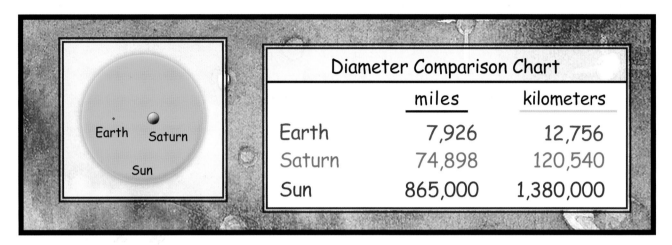

Diameter Comparison Chart		
	miles	kilometers
Earth	7,926	12,756
Saturn	74,898	120,540
Sun	865,000	1,380,000

The diameter (length of a straight line going through the center of a planet, star, or across the widest part of a circle) of Saturn is a little more than nine times greater than the diameter of Earth.

Checklist of Items needed:
- A paper plate that measures just over 9 inches when flattened out
- A ruler
- A pencil
- A quarter (the diameter of a quarter equals one inch)

Directions:
- Using a ruler, draw a line across the "fattest" part of the plate. It should be just a hair over nine inches. This is the diameter of your circle.
- Starting at either end of line, place the fat part of a quarter on the line and trace around it.
- Repeat this, placing the quarters right next to each other so that you have nine traces of quarters.

Looking at the statement above, what does your paper plate circle represent and what does one of the quarters represent?

Saturn is the second largest planet in the solar system. Jupiter is bigger!

The plate represents Saturn and a quarter represents the Earth

Temperature:

The average temperature on Saturn is about ⁻220F or ⁻140C.
Does that mean it is warmer or colder than freezing on Saturn?
What temperature is it in your house or school?
What temperature is it outside today? Is it above or below freezing?
What is the average temperature where you live during the winter?
At what temperature does water freeze and become ice?

Density:

Saturn is the only planet in the solar system that's less dense than water. That means if you could find a tub big enough to hold it, Saturn would float!

What are some other things that can float?

Distances:

Saturn is about 888 million miles from the sun.
Saturn is approximately 795 million miles away from the Earth, when they are both on the same side of the sun at its closest point of approach.

Saturn's Moons:

Saturn has forty-seven moons and scientists keep finding more. Thirty-four of the moons have names. They are Albiorix, Atlas, Calypso, Dione, Enceladus, Epimetheus, Erriapo, Helene, Hyperion, Iapetus, Ijiraq, Janus, Kiviuq, Methone, Mimas, Mundilfari, Narvi, Paaliaq, Pallene, Pan, Pandora, Phoebe, Polydeuces, Prometheus, Rhea, Siarnaq, Skadi, Suttung, Tarvos, Telesto, Tethys, Thrym, Titan, and Ymir. The moons don't make their own light but they "glow" by reflecting the light from the sun—just like our moon does.

Saturn's Rings

Saturn has *seven major rings*. They are listed as D, C, B, A, F, G, & E. The rings are made up of billions of water ice particles.

The rings are not solid. In fact, they are floating pieces of ice and rock that are "held together" by the gravity from both Saturn and its many moons. The rocks vary in size from as small as a grain of sand to as big as a half-mile wide. The ice won't melt because it is so cold.

The rings look big and wide but they are really narrow: some are only a half-mile thick. Next time you get in the car, ask the driver to help you measure a half mile.

Edible Rings

The ice & rock mix that make up Saturn's rings are like rings of dirty, hard-packed snow.

Checklist of What you will need:

Ice cream to represent the ice

Nuts – finely chopped to coarsely chopped to represent the rocks of all sizes

A small plate and plastic wrap that fits loosely over the plate.

Let the ice cream soften enough to stir in the nuts. Put the ice cream around the inside rim of the plate so that it makes a ring. Cover the plate with the plastic and put in the freezer until solid. When frozen, you have your edible Saturn rings!

What would happen to your ring if you put it in the oven?

What would happen to Saturn's rings if it started getting hot?